Barry the Penguin's Black and White Christmas

A MUSICAL BY LESLEY ROSS & JOHN-VICTOR

Adapted by RACHEL BELLMAN with LESLEY ROSS

Illustrations by MATT ROWE

Narrated By
CHRISTOPHER ECCLESTON

CD Cast (In order of appearance)

Barry the Penguin
HAYDN OAKLEY

Phoebe
KATE HUME

Queen of the Bed Bugs
KERRY ELLIS

Close the Elf
MICHAEL XAVIER

Father Christmas
RICARDO AFONSO

Sister Actavia
LOUISE JAMESON

The Wordsmith
GABRIEL VICK

CD included. See ~~back page for~~ full recording credits.

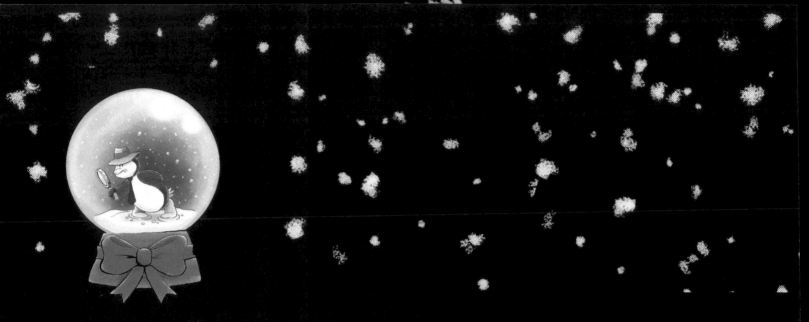

Lesley Ross - Playwright and Lyricist

Lesley Ross has been writing theatre for young people ever since he can remember. Highlights include: *The Little Tempest* for the National Theatre, *The Ghana Dream* for Theatre Royal Plymouth, *Rameo & Eweliet* for the Unknown Theatre. Also seven family musicals about the adventures of the Super Sheep - *The Sheep Chronicles*, as well as *Jorinda & Jorindel - An Elephant's Adventure* for the Welsh National Opera, *Hansel & Gretel* for Simply Theatre Geneva, *Rumpelstiltskin* for Everyman Theatre Cardiff, and the play *The Unfortunate Tale of An Egg* for Theatre Royal York. Like Barry, he loves fish, music and saving the world and he would like to dedicate this book to all his godchildren (and his odd-children): Caitlin, Zoe, Jack, Ethan, Mollie, Carmel, Lauren, Poppy, Scarlett, Harry, Fran, Rebekah, Eli, Hannah, Finn, Daniel, Scooby, Juno, and of course... Phoebe! @lesleyrosslyric

John-Victor - Composer

John-Victor is a UK born songwriter, classically trained since the age of six. He has just released his debut album *Shoot...Bang!* Two of his musicals featured on the album are being developed by Perfect Pitch, including *Barry The Penguin's Black and White Christmas* which is his first full length musical. @JohnVictorMusic

Rachel Bellman - Author

Rachel Bellman is Literary Associate of Perfect Pitch, a not-for-profit theatre company that collaborates with creatives worldwide to create high quality new British musicals. She grew up in London, studied English at Oxford University, and wrote her first (unpublished) novel aged 13 which she still keeps under her bed. Rachel is also currently working on her first full musical *Flower Cutters*. @RachelBellman

Matt Rowe - Illustrator

Illustrator Matt Rowe lives and works in Worcestershire and has been freelancing for 13 years. Initially specialising in cartoony greetings cards, his passion has been to illustrate children's books. His first published work came in 2013 as illustrator for the book entitled *Arvor's School Days*.

"This book is great fun, a mad and humorous adaptation of an original new musical. It has been an absolute pleasure to be a part of this unique project and I look forward to seeing it all on the stage one day."

Christopher Eccleston

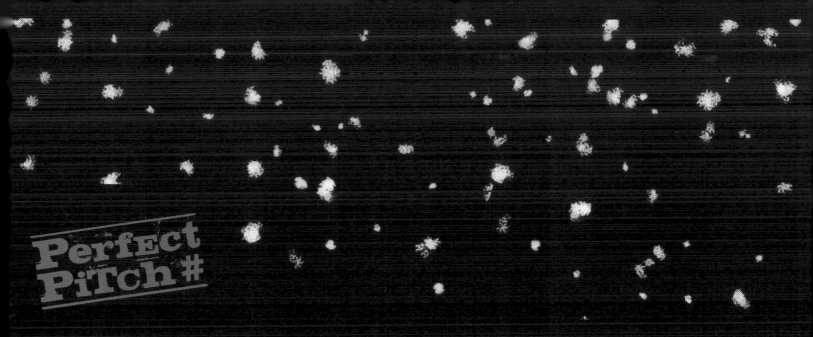

Perfect Pitch is a not-for-profit theatre company dedicated to the development of new British musicals. In 2010 we approached playwright/lyricist Lesley Ross and composer John-Victor and invited them to work alongside us to create an exciting new family Christmas musical. They returned to us a few months later with an idea for a magical story about penguins, nuns, bedbugs, a confused Santa and the beginnings of a lively pop/rock score. They had us at "Barry the Penguin"!

We have been developing the full scale musical in collaboration with a host of different performers, producers, directors and musical directors and it is now ready and awaiting its premiere stage production. In the meantime we wanted to create this wonderful children's book complete with songs to read-a-long, sing-a-long and dance-a-long to! The idea to have the stage musical adapted into a picture and audio book was inspired by our own children Hayden and Max so we dedicate this book to them!

To #followthepenguin and the journey of the stage musical visit our website www.perfectpitchmusicals.com and follow us on twitter @perfectpitch. We hope you enjoy *Barry the Penguin's Black and White Christmas* as much as we do!

Andy Barnes & Wendy Barnes
Producers of Perfect Pitch

Supported using public funding by
ARTS COUNCIL ENGLAND

"Perfect Pitch, who are an extraordinary organisation, see, nurture, develop, and incubate ideas for musicals… I think we sometimes forget in Britain just how extraordinarily good we are at musicals."

Stephen Fry, Patron of Perfect Pitch

Matador
9 Priory Business Park,
Wistow Road, Kibworth Beauchamp,
Leicestershire. LE8 0RX
Tel: 0116 279 2299
Email: books@troubador.co.uk
Web: www.troubador.co.uk/matador
Twitter: @matadorbooks

ISBN 978 1784623 579

British Library Cataloguing in Publication Data.
A catalogue record for this book is available from the British Library.

Printed and bound by CPI Group (UK) Ltd, Croydon, CR0 4YY

Matador is an imprint of Troubador Publishing Ltd

FSC MIX
Paper from
responsible sources
FSC® C013604

We welcome all to hear this story told,
December twenty-third will be the date.
The night a great adventure will unfold,
The night a penguin seals a human's fate.

Written in The Penguin Book of Prophecy

Phoebe Foster **hated** Christmas.
She **hated** Christmas carols,
she **hated** Brussels sprouts,
and she **hated** mince pies too

More than anything **she hated Father Christmas!**
Or rather, she no longer believed in him.

Despite this Phoebe still kept one special Christmas present.
The one her dad gave her when she was little. Phoebe still
remembered how excited she was when she saw the box wrapped
up one Christmas morning.

"To my Little Bee, love Daddy."

Inside this very special box was a snow globe.
And inside the snow globe was a tiny penguin.

But sadly Phoebe's dad had died when she was just a little girl. That year she was so upset she wrote a letter to Father Christmas.

"Please, let me be his Little Bee again.
Just one more time."

Afterwards she tried to be nice and never naughty, listening to her mum and eating her vegetables. Even Brussels sprouts! But when Christmas morning arrived her dad was nowhere to be seen. She waited all day, and believed with all her heart that her wish would be granted. But she never saw her dad. And so she never wanted anything else from Father Christmas ever again. She no longer believed in him.

Then one year, on the night before Christmas Eve, something very strange happened. Phoebe had fallen asleep on the sofa. Suddenly the window slid open and a gust of cold winter air swept through the room, making the curtains flutter.

Then a penguin squeezed through the window!

He examined the tree,
 inspected the presents,
  and tried on the tinsel.

Finally he caught sight of a tattered old box, tucked away in the corner. He waddled over and saw the snow globe inside. In shock, he fell into the tree.

Phoebe woke up. "Mum?" The bird stared back at her. "Penguin! Why is there a penguin in my living room?"

"Penguin has a name actually," the penguin said.

"What?"

"Barry. Barry, The Penguin."

Barry was a penguin detective! He told Phoebe that Father Christmas had been kidnapped, and that The Penguin Book of Prophecy said there was one child in all the world who could save him.

"And all the clues point to you, Peebee Foster. It's really quite simple."

"It's Phoebe."

"Peebee Foster, you are the chosen one who will save Christmas!"

Phoebe was dumbfounded. "I don't believe in Christmas, so I know I'm not chosen for anything."

"Then why do you have one of the Three Magic Gifts?"

"The three what?"

Phoebe had no idea what Barry was talking about. Then he held up the snow globe, the one that her dad had given her. She tried to explain that it wasn't magic. He shook the globe. Phoebe felt a chill, and looked up.

White snowflakes were drifting down through her living room.

"See. Magic." Barry started to leave.

"Where are you going?"

"To the secret river!"

SONG: Follow the Penguin

There's no more time for explanation.
Please entertain my small request.
Is this the season for your questions
When you're the reason for this quest?

Follow the penguin,
And see the world in black and white.
Follow the penguin,
And we will put this world to right.

Because out in the mist,
No doubting the distant
Path we're meant to follow
-ing the penguin,
Flipping out into the night!

So... go on and grab your gumshoe flippers,
Zip up your fears, unclip your mind,
And we will crack this case together,
But first *be bold and brave and blindly*

Follow the penguin,
And see the world in black and white,
Follow the penguin,
And we will put this world to right.

Phoebe followed Barry through the streets, until they were standing above a manhole in the road.

"Behold!" Barry ran towards the hole in the ground. "It's the secret river!"

"What? Down in the sewer?" Phoebe peeked in. There, undeniably, was a magical stream, with silver water rushing by. "Okay, that's pretty cool. But what now?"

"To the North Pole!" Barry flexed his flippers and prepared to jump.

"Um… okay then."

Dive in the water and show me 'The Fin',
Do what you oughta, never give in!
Alright, dive in the water and show me 'The Fin',
Do what you oughta, never give in!

Gotta swim, gotta swim, flipping out, diving in,
For the answer is out there, where we gotta swim.

NO MORE REGRET! LET'S JUST GET WET!

Feel the water start to carry Barry the Penguin,
Flipping out into the sea.
Because Barry's the best, he's leading the quest
To the crime scene 'vestigation!
Like a penguin!
Flipping out to follow me,
Flipping out into the sea,

Flipping out, detectives we!

While Barry and Phoebe headed to the North Pole, Father Christmas was waking up at the South Pole, deep in the depths of Antarctica.

"Where am I? What is this place?"

A glamorous and ghastly creature approached.

"Oh, hello there. I say, you're a bed bug, aren't you? But you're bigger.

Much, much BIGGER!"

"I am the Queen of the Bed Bugs. Welcome to the South Pole, your new home! Here you will help me infest and infect Christmas with millions and billions of bed bugs.

Together we will turn Christmas naughty, not nice."

"NEVER!"

Father Christmas panicked. It was Christmas Eve! How could he prepare the presents if he was stuck at the wrong pole?

He made a scramble for the icy exit.

But the Bed Bug Queen blocked his way with her many legs. She cackled her evil bed bug laugh.

"Here at the South Pole everything's upside down. Opposite your distant Northern home you will become the upside-down-opposite of what you are. By the time midnight strikes… Good Santa will be Bad Santa! And then this world will be mine!"

Back in the North Pole, Phoebe looked around the toy workshop, at the thousands of sweets and presents piled high to the ceiling.

"Are you sure this is the North Pole, Barry? Shouldn't there be elves working here or something? Barry?"

"Behold! The famous Christmas machine!" Barry pointed to a massive button with a flourish, skidding to the centre of the room. "Only Father Christmas can work it, and when he presses it at midnight, all Christmas will start.

It is majestic…

It is all powerful…

And it is called… THE BUTTON."

"Shouldn't we be looking for Father Christmas?" asked Phoebe.

"Right, yeah." Barry began hunting through the presents. "Examine the scene. Detective head: on." He looked at the floor. "Aha! A footprint. This could be a clue."

"That's my footprint."

"Then we can eliminate it!" Barry preened triumphantly.

Phoebe asked Barry about The Penguin Book of Prophecy. "Does the book say if Father Christmas will be saved?"

"That, Little Bee, is up to you."

"Don't call me that." Phoebe was upset.

'Little Bee' was the name her dad used to call her. She hugged her snow globe tightly. "Just tell me about the Prophecy."

"Well, the Book says that a child called Peebee Foster will need THREE MAGIC GIFTS. There's the LIQUID, to show what needs to be seen, the OBJECT, to defeat the rise of evil, and the WORD, to right the terrible wrongs. You've already got the object, so…"

Barry was interrupted by an elf, dashing through the workshop.

"Much work to do. Much bad to stop. Please help Close. Help, help, help."

"Don't make a move," Barry whispered. "I know Kung fu."

The elf said his name was Close. "She came. The bad bug came and stole Father. Now there's no one to push The Button!"

When they told him they would help, Close stared at Phoebe. "He knew you would come." Then Close revealed a glass bottle.

SONG: Snow Waltz

Father's gone but Close will stay,
Close the door til the prophecy day.
Come close and see the present, be strong.
Presently will you *bring back our song?*

Elves would dance,
Elves would sing,
Elves are laughing at father the king.
Arctic workshop full of joy,
Building gifts for a girl or a boy...

All have left,
Close alone,
Still one seed that is left to be sewn.
A second gift that's just for you,
Just and noble,
But what will you do?

Close gave the bottle to Phoebe and warned them, "Midnight is coming. You must find the WORD. Save Christmas! Find the Wordsmith."

Close scurried away, and Phoebe wondered where on earth this Wordsmith was. She looked at the glass bottle. It was glowing.

"Hey! It's the LIQUID, the MAGIC GIFT to show what needs to be seen!" Barry stared into the light, and Phoebe passed it to him. "How does it work?"

But the glass was so slippery in his flippers that Barry dropped the bottle, and it smashed. The liquid spilled all over the floor, spitting and sizzling and fizzling. Suddenly they saw a hole forming beneath them and they realised it was pulling and sucking them into the ground!

SONG: Going Underground

It's getting thin beneath my feet.
I think my *body's* heading underground.
I hope my skin don't overheat...
I'm used to water, can we please turn around?

There's something pulling,
There's something pulling us.
Underground! Under ground ground!

Take my hand. (I'm starting to squirm!)
Through the land. (I wish I was a worm!)
Make a stand. (I think I saw a rabbit!)

We're going underground! Going underground!
We're going underground! Going underground!

Going deep, yeah we're going real deep.
Take a leap, cos we're getting real steep,
Deeper still, like a pneumatic drill.

We're going underground, going underground!
We're going underground, going underground!

Going deep and away from the sun,
Take a leap cos we're having some fun,
Unaware what is taking us there!

We're going underground, going underground, we're going underground,
going underground, going underground.
UNDERGROUND!

Barry and Phoebe found themselves deep inside the Centre of the Earth. After wandering through the web of tunnels, they realised they were lost.
'

Then, a nun appeared!

"Well, hellooo there! We've been looking all over for you two." She held a plate of sandwiches and a bazooka. "This is for creating more tunnels. So much easier than digging them. And the sandwiches? Well… wait a minute… oh yes, these are for you. Unless of course you'd prefer a vegetarian lasagne." The nun was called Actavia. "Rumour has it, the Bed Bug Queen is gathering an army. Nasty creatures, bed bugs, and only nine hours left to save Christmas. So it's best you meet the Wordsmith, and soon. Don't worry though, he won't kill you now, not if you're the chosen one. You are the chosen one, are you not?"

"Well…" Phoebe looked at Barry. But he was staring at Actavia, his cheeks flushed and his feathers fluffed.
"You're a silent one. Catfish got your tongue? Or is it a penguin thing? Never seen a penguin before, but I saw a polar bear once. Very grumpy lot, polar bears, but show them a good romance and you'll soon see the polar bears smiling. Now, where's that map?" Actavia left through a tunnel.

Phoebe asked if Barry was feeling all right.

"That is the most beautiful penguin I have ever seen in my short and rather uneventful life."

"Barry, she's not a penguin. She's a nun."

"What sort of bird is that? Oh dear. Do you think a nun bird could ever love a penguin bird?"

"No... well, maybe."

Barry sighed into the distance. "Maybe."

SONG: The Polar Bears are Smiling

If she'd only heard
The way my heart went flipper.
I'm a lonely *bird*
Who needs to share his kipper!
And the ice,
And the ice,
And the ice will thaw,
Yes the ice will thaw.
I'm sure the price is worth it all.

She's the one who doesn't scare me...
All *in* black and white,
All the greater to ensnare me,
She's my guiding light.
Through the storm and the strife,
For the whole of my life,
I'll *believe* that fish can fly.
Cos the polar *bears* are smiling!

We'll be black and white together,
Make my wish come true,
I will fish this world forever,
Always next to you.
I will be your one,
You're my first *bar* none!
The seals are dancing wild.
And the polar bears are smiling!
All the polar bears are smiling!
Yes the polar bears are smiling...

Phoebe told Barry to focus. They had to see the Wordsmith, but according to Actavia he was dangerous.

"We've got to do this right or else you, Barry the penguin detective, and I, Phoebe Elizabeth Foster, could be killed!"

"Wait, what did you say your name was?"

"Phoebe Elizabeth Foster."

"And by that do you mean your initials aren't P. B.?"

"They're not. That was my dad, Paul Benjamin Foster."

"Oh dear."

When Phoebe asked what Barry meant, he said that he may have made the biggest blunder in the history of the brainless bird. "Back when we met, I called you P. B. Foster, and you said 'It's Phoebe'. I thought you had the right name, the one from The Penguin Book of Prophecy. But I think I got it wrong. I think the chosen one was your dad, not you."

Phoebe stared at him in horror. "But my dad is dead."

"I know," Barry replied. "We're doomed."

Meanwhile the Bed Bug Queen's plan was working. The more time Father Christmas spent in the South Pole, the more he became the terrible opposite of what he was supposed to be. Spread through the icy cave were presents that he and the Queen would send across the world at midnight. Except instead of toys, these presents contained bed bug eggs! The Queen approached.

"Look!" Father Christmas unveiled a monstrous machine. It was like the one Barry and Phoebe had seen at the North Pole, but this one was horrible and rotten. It was ready to deliver the bed bug infested presents. "I call it… **Bad Button**."

"Oh, Daddy C, you've made me very happy."

Father Christmas liked his new name. Then the Queen told him that a penguin and a girl called Phoebe were on their way to ruin his plans. He felt the darkness of the South Pole calling to him from within.

SONG: Upside Down

When those sleigh bells are ringing
And they start their singing,
Like a wasp, I go stinging them all.
What I see before me
Is the key to the glory
As I rewrite the story for all.

So, the nature of you
Will help us all push through,
So tell us what to do with the girl?

Daddy C knows what to do,
Father Christmas, toodleloo,
That is how the daddy rocks,
So wrap the girl up in a box.
Snap a penguin into three,
Dip the bits into your tea,
For Daddy C, he wears the crown,
Time to turn this whole world upside down!
Upside down!

For Daddy C will break the mould,
Break this present stranglehold,
Christmas time has had its day so let's try another way.
Come on pay the Daddy price,
Bless the naughty not the nice.
It's enough to break your heart
When you see your world get ripped apart.
RIPPED APART! RIPPED APART!
RIPPED APART!

Back in the Centre of the Earth, Phoebe and Barry were on their way to meet the Wordsmith. They were terrified. How could the Book be wrong? How could they save the world if the chosen one was actually Phoebe's father?

They arrived at a seething lake of lava. Barry pulled out a magnifying glass.

"Yep. That could kill us alright. Shall we go back?" They heard a voice. "Hello. Welcome to my lake." The Wordsmith appeared before them. "Lake: four letters, eight points."

"What is with the points?"

Phoebe explained to Barry that the Wordsmith was talking about a game her father used to love, a game with words.

"So, you want my MAGIC WORD? Gift number three? But to get Gift number three, you'll have to answer three questions."

If she really was the chosen one, the Wordsmith said, they would pass the test. But if they failed, he would throw them into the lava. Before Phoebe could decide what to do, the Wordsmith began...

"QUESTION ONE: What date is Christmas Eve?"
Phoebe couldn't believe her luck.

"The 24th of December." Barry stared in amazement.

"You think you're clever do you? Well, try QUESTION TWO: Which reindeer has a red nose?" Barry turned to Phoebe in panic. But the answer came to her in a heartbeat.

"Rudolph?" She was right again! The Wordsmith did not look happy. "Bring on QUESTION THREE."

"How many points in the word Christmas?"
Phoebe was stumped.

"I have no idea."

"No idea? Ha! Have a clue. Clue: four letters, six points." He waved his arm, and letters and numbers appeared in the lake:

The letter C was missing. Phoebe counted thirteen points without it, and added on what she thought C was worth. But she and Barry had different answers.

Barry felt in his penguin heart that C was four.

"Barry, you're the detective. And I trust you. We'll go with your answer: seventeen."

"That is… the WRONG answer." Phoebe's heart sank. Then the Wordsmith said they had PASSED the test. "I never said you had to answer RIGHT, I said you must prove you are the chosen one. Only the chosen one would trust a penguin with their life. I can now tell you that the WORD is:

"EVILI?"

"The heart is missing, and the chosen one is the key. Look to the past. Save the future!"

The Wordsmith vanished with a flash.

Phoebe wondered if she would ever solve the puzzle if she wasn't the chosen one. But they had all three Gifts. What could they do but go to the South Pole?

There were now six hours left until midnight, and the Bed Bug Queen was calling her army.

"Come, my scuttling, scurrying servants. When the clock strikes midnight Daddy C will press the Bad Button, and then it will unleash my shimmering brood of hatching bed bugs! Behold the birth of our beautiful domination!"

SONG: Rise

What's that filthy smell of almond
Fest'ring in the dark?
Could it be the smell of evil waiting to disembark?
Many years we've hidden and we've
Waited for our chance.
Now no more forbidden steps,
We're coming, time to dance!

We'll rise rise rise,
Rise rise rise,
We'll rise rise, rise again tonight!

There's an army in their thousands
When you crawl into your bed,
You enthral them with your slumber,
Slow and sluggish, sleepyhead.
In the dead of night they're waiting
For the dawning of their need,
So there's no more hesitating
When it's time for us to feed.

So, when you go and hit the switch,
Then our bodies start to twitch,
For your blood it will enrich,
That's the when and where and which,
Why we hitch another ride,
In your present gonna hide,
Til your bedroom we reside,
Biding time until the switch,
Then you're gonna itch!

So we march a mighty army
And we bleed this middle world,
First we EAT the Penguin puppet
Then we FEED upon the Girl!
If these nuns protest, infest their halls
And bring them to their end!
For tonight's the night they'll see
The bed bug finally ascend.

I will rise up! See me rising!
Soon I'll rise up! Soon!
Rise!
Rise!
Tonight!

Barry and Phoebe packed their things and got ready to go to the South Pole. Actavia gave them peanuts squashed by buttered bricks. "It's butternut squash!" All of a sudden, they heard a scurrying sound echo through the caverns. It grew louder, like an approaching tidal wave. Actavia picked up the bazooka. "Phoebe, I'd load this up if I were you."

Bed bugs started crawling through the cracks in the rock. Hundreds, thousands. The shadow of the Bed Bug Queen towered behind the mighty army. Barry used his Kung fu while Phoebe used the bazooka to blast the bed bugs back into the tunnels. But there were too many. They were being bitten all over, and they could hear the Queen laughing.

Phoebe thought she had failed. The real chosen one would not lose the battle! Then she heard Barry's voice calling to her.

"Phoebe! Remember the Prophecy." Phoebe remembered her dad's snow globe: 'the MAGIC OBJECT, to defeat the rise of evil.'

She shook it, and snow started falling.

"Bed bugs hate the cold. Get them!" Phoebe smashed the globe against the rock, and a freezing blizzard swept through the Centre of the Earth. The bed bug army scuttled away, defeated.

Phoebe and Actavia were left with piles of snow melting on their heads, while Barry did a backflip and flapped his flippers. "We won!"

Phoebe smiled. "For now at least." Barry gazed at her in wonder.

"Maybe you are the chosen one after all."

She looked down at the snow globe. Her dad's gift had saved them, as if he'd been looking out for her all along.

"I don't think it matters if my name's in a book or not. If I can do this, I'll do it for my dad."

SONG: The Girl Inside of Me

My father always said if life throws lemons,
Then lemonade is what you learn to pour.
But when the fruit is bitter
Don't you throw the lemons back?
I need to find the strength to win this war.

There are days when you are lonely,
Endless days no longer free.
But then a penguin comes along and changes your whole life.
I found… the girl inside of me.

Because a magic globe
Can sometimes make it snow,
And *bad* things come along, but then in time they go.
I'll *be* the girl my father hoped I'd be,
I'll *brave* this fight for Christmas,
I will save this night for Christmas,
I know I must save Christmas
For the girl inside of me!

What I lost when I was small
I've found a way now through it all.
No turning back, this is our cause,
We will not fail, we will not pause,
Tonight we're gonna fight the fight for Santa Claus!

Now it's time to turn the tide!
With this penguin by my side!
I won't hide
The girl inside of me.
Inside of me.
Inside of me!

Less than an hour before midnight, Phoebe and Barry journeyed to the South Pole. When they burst into the ice cave, they saw the evil machine that Father Christmas had built. Then the man himself stepped out of the shadows, dressed in black.

"Father Christmas!"

"The name is Daddy C." He turned to Phoebe. "I know you. You're the girl who doesn't believe. The girl who hates Christmas."

"That's not true." Phoebe told him that she used to hate Christmas, but now she understood what she couldn't understand before. "I asked you for something that I already had. My dad still loves me, wherever he is, and I know he'll always be here."

Father Christmas pondered in front of the machine.

"You need to believe in yourself! Remember who you really are!"

Just then, the Bed Bug Queen arrived. "Go on, Daddy C. Push that button! End it!"

Father Christmas looked at Phoebe. "You're right, Phoebe. I cannot do it." He stepped away from the button. The Queen started laughing. As her evil laugh pierced through them a wall of ice shattered, revealing Actavia, captured, trapped in a cage of icicles.

"Push the button, or I'll kill the nun!"

They stared in shock. Barry looked heartbroken. All Phoebe knew was they couldn't let Actavia die. Father Christmas lifted his hand.

"I'm counting on you now, child." He pressed the Bad Button. The hideous machine whirred into action. Any minute the presents containing the bed bug eggs would be sent to children all around the world.

"Finally! My fatal future can begin. Now to gnaw on the neck of this nun!"

Barry rushed to save Actavia but the Queen turned and attacked him.

"Barry, watch out!"

Phoebe and the others charged at her. But it wasn't enough! She was still biting at the little penguin. Then Phoebe noticed a tiny crack in the ice, next to the machine.

"Barry!" Phoebe pointed, and Barry moved towards the patch of thin ice as he wrestled.

"Penguin pest!" The Queen lurched forward to bite Barry's neck, but he moved out of the way, and she hit the ground with all her weight. Crack! The ice split into pieces, and the Queen of the Bed Bugs found herself dangling just above the freezing water. Barry held her by one leg.

"If there's one thing I know about bed bugs… they can't swim!" Barry let go. The Queen fell with a horrendous screech, down, into the water, beneath the ice.

She was gone.

The group cheered, but the machine was still going. As they watched, midnight started to chime.

Barry stumbled, weakened from the fight.

"Actavia... do you think you could you ever love... a penguin?"

"Oh, my sweet bird. You know I can never marry. But if you get through this, I'll happily spend the rest of my life with you, my dear penguin friend."

Phoebe watched Barry collapse into Actavia's arms. "This isn't how it's supposed to end." Barry dropped his head and closed his eyes. "No... I'm not the chosen one. That's the problem, isn't it? I've failed everyone."

Father Christmas patted her shoulder. "It's alright *Little Bee*, you did your best."

Suddenly, Barry lifted his head. "What did he just call her? Little Bee?" Barry jumped to his feet. "Oh my word. The third magic gift, Phoebe. The WORD!

E V I L I"

Phoebe was at a loss. "But I don't know how to use it."

"No, no, no! The **heart** is missing. The **chosen one** is the key! There are letters missing. Your name, the one your dad gave you when you still loved Christmas. B-E-E. Rearrange the word!"

Barry drew the letters in the snow, so that

became…

I BELIEVE

"Barry, you're the greatest detective that ever lived!" Phoebe hugged Barry tight.

"You need to say the magic words, Phoebe," Barry said through her hug. "Right the terrible wrongs."

"Say them now, say them now!" Actavia clung to Barry's flipper.

Phoebe shut her eyes, and understood with all her heart. She was still her dad's Little Bee. She always would be. She spoke loud and clear: "I *believe!*"

The clamorous clanking of colossal cogs and wheels echoed all around. And the evil Christmas machine creaked to a halt.

"You did it, Bee, you saved the world!"

"No Barry, we did it."

As Phoebe spoke, the ice around her started to swirl and spin. Father Christmas and Actavia faded out of her vision. The walls of Phoebe's living room began to replace the South Pole.

Phoebe held onto Barry for dear life.

"It's time to say goodbye, Phoebe."

"Oh, Barry the Penguin. I'll never forget you."

Phoebe woke up. She was back on her sofa, and for a terrible moment Phoebe was afraid that everything had been a dream. Then a familiar figure waddled in, all restored to tip top, flip flop health.

"Barry!"

He was carrying a present for her.

"Father Christmas would have brought it, but I wanted to do the honours my own feathered self." Phoebe unwrapped the gift, and beneath the paper was a snow globe.

"It's beautiful."

"And that's not all it is," said Actavia as she danced into the room. "You ever want to see how we are, just shake that little globe and we'll appear like a good old habit."

Barry took Actavia's hand.

"And for the record, I always knew you were the chosen one. Turns out us penguins don't use the name Elizabeth. We just use 'Beth'. Phoebe Beth. P. B. Foster. Amazing!"

After one last hug, the black and white best friends prepared to depart. Phoebe gazed inside the globe as outside it started to snow.

SONG: Believe Again

When I look back upon this day,
All of the things I used to say,
All of the dreams that seemed to fade...
All of the time so unaware
All of my father's love was there, all of my life.

And now I believe again, I feel it in every way,
I will believe again, the marvel of this day.
But I won't regret a moment,
And I'm glad I questioned why,
For I believe again,
Believe again... in Christmas time.

A day that can flip you from the place you were before,
It's trippy, it's sometimes like a dream.
But still there's a truth within you simply can't ignore.
You find out just what a day can mean.

And I *believe again*, with every *beat* of my *heart*,
Yes I *believe again*, the world may fall apart
But here with you *beside* me, this year will *be* okay.
Cos I *believe again*, *believe again*. In Christmas Day.

Believe again in joy and love and peace and hope,
In the different ways I need to cope,
In penguins who can show their worth,
In crazy nuns who live at the Centre of the Earth,
In fathers who love you
Even though you know that they have gone,
In life and love and joy and even in this song,

BELIEVE AGAIN IN CHRISTMAS DAY!

Barry the Penguin would like to thank...

All the performers and creatives that have helped in the development
of the show of which there are too many to mention but he knows who
you all are and is always grateful for your valuable input!

Also special thanks to Sam Featherstone, Ryan McBryde,
Paul Herbert, Josh Bird, Simon Greiff, Mandy Hare,
Ros Povey & Zoe Simpson and in particular his penguin
chums Jack Shalloo & Haydn Oakley.

Don't forget to #followthepenguin
on twitter @BARRY PENGUIN

AUDIO CD

Track 1: The Penguin Book of Prophecy
Track 2: Follow the Penguin
Track 3: Snow Waltz
Track 4: Underground
Track 5: The Polar Bears are Smiling
Track 6: Upside Down
Track 7: Rise
Track 8: The Girl Inside of Me
Track 9: Believe Again

Price Studios

Audio recorded at Price Studios, London
Produced by Sam Featherstone
Mixed by John-Victor and Sam Featherstone
Orchestrations and underscore composed and produced by John-Victor
Voiceover director: Gregory Ashton
Backing Vocalists: Jackie-Ross Lavender and Sophie Adkins
Backing Vocalists for "The Polar Bears are Smiling": CiCi Howells and Charlotte Layne